Keepin' Her Man

Shay Jackson

SADDLEBACK
EDUCATIONAL PUBLISHING

Bein' Good

Blind Trust

Fitting In

Holding Back

Keepin' Her Man

EDUCATIONAL PUBLISHING
www.sdlback.com

ISBN-13: 978-1-61651-774-8
ISBN-10: 1-61651-774-3
eBook: 978-1-61247-336-9

Printed in Guangzhou, China
1111/CA21101798

16 15 14 13 12   1 2 3 4 5

Marnyke and Kiki sat at their usual table. It was study hall, their last class of the day. Kiki was trying to finish her math homework before it was time for yearbook club. Marnyke, of course, was not studying.

"What you doin' tonight, Kiki? Homework, right?" Marnyke asked.

Kiki smiled. "Yeah, probably," she admitted. "After YC, that is. You're going, right?"

"To yearbook club? Not tonight," Marnyke said. "I've gotta get ready. Goin' over to Darnell's place later."

Kiki shook her head.

"His mom's gonna be gone, Kiki."

Kiki set her pencil down. "Oh, yeah?" she asked.

Marnyke nodded. "Uh-huh," she said, flipping her pencil back and forth nervously. "I'm startin' to think, you know, that it's time."

"Do you trust him?" Kiki asked. "You haven't been together long."

Marnyke smiled. "Long enough, I think. I think it's just the way of things, Kiki. I gotta do it. I'll lose him if I don't."

"What do you mean?" Kiki asked.

"I mean, I think that's why he's been so distant lately," Marnyke replied.

The last bell rang before Kiki could respond. Marnyke grabbed her purse and stood up carefully. "Damn," she groaned.

"What?" Kiki asked with concern.

"Oh, these shoes. It's my first time wearing 'em for a whole day."

"That's what you get," Kiki said. "Look at those things! How can you even walk?"

Marnyke put her hand on Kiki's shoulder. "We can't all look cute in sneakers," she said. "Some of us have to try a little harder than others."

"Well, I can't be your crutch. *I'm* going to YC, remember?" Kiki said.

"I know, I know. I don't like to be seen with you in the halls anyway," Marnyke joked. "Go on. I'll holler at ya later."

"Later," Kiki said with a smile. Then she hustled out of the classroom and down the hall.

Marnyke, on the other hand, took small, calculated steps. The problem was the right shoe. It had started hurting second period. The whole back of Marnyke's right heel was rubbed raw.

But this wasn't her first time in tough heels. She knew how to pull it off, even if they were killing her. She'd walked twenty city blocks in shoes worse than these before. The key was to walk slowly and take small steps. Swing your hips. That way no one notices the limp, they just see how good you look.

The shoes looked amazing. They were shiny, strappy, and cherry red, with a three-inch heel. The straps went up high on the ankle and looked great with skinny jeans. Marnyke got them at the discount store on Seventh Street. It was her favorite shop. The buyer there knew what she was doing, and the prices were solid.

Marnyke loved their stuff too, because she'd never seen anyone at school wearing the same things. And that's how Marnyke liked it. Style mattered, and Marnyke definitely had style. So did her red, strappy shoes.

She just had to break 'em in. She grabbed her huge sunglasses out of her bag and put them on. You never knew who was watching. She threw her notebook and pencil into her locker and grabbed her jacket. She was out of there for the day.

Marnyke felt a little bad about ditching YC today. It was almost the only thing about school she liked. Everyone would wonder why she wasn't there. She didn't care. She tossed her jacket over her shoulder and moved with the crowd of students toward the exit.

There was a bus that went from the school to her neighborhood, but Marnyke liked the subway better. She walked slowly to the subway entrance. Then she leaned on the handrail a little as she went down the steps.

Once underground, she felt relieved. She could give her feet a little rest when she got on the train! Her train arrived and slowed to a stop. She spied a seat and moved toward it quickly. No way was she going to stand.

The steady sway of the subway always relaxed her. It felt good to be moving away from that stupid school. Plus, someone left a fashion magazine on the seat next to her. It was a good one too, about an inch thick. Marnyke grabbed it and stuck it in her bag. She wanted to look through it right then. But she worried that whoever forgot it might want it back. So she kept it hidden in her bag.

The train approached her stop. It was downtown. Marnyke stood up and walked toward the doors. This was her favorite part of every school day. She loved walking home through downtown. She usually got there around 4:00, right when the suits started pouring out of their offices. True, the suits were all on their way home to some better hood or suburb. But that didn't matter to Marnyke. What mattered was turning heads.

Maybe it was her hair, in its perfectly round and bouncy Afro. Maybe it was her mile-long legs. Whatever it was, men and women alike seemed to look at her a moment longer than they should. She just had that way about her. She loved the attention too. It was the best part of her day.

But, as always, the magic ended around Twenty-third Street. That's where downtown ended and midtown began. Midtown was the industrial area of the city. At this time of day, the shops, restaurants, and offices were still open. But not for long. Midtown became a ghost town after 7:00.

Midtown was full of huge high-rise complexes with inexpensive apartments. Marnyke lived in one of them.

Her building was nothing special. But it was a lot better than the dive Marnyke used to live in. That was when she lived with her mom before things got really out of control.

Marnyke lived with her older sister Akira now. The building was kind of old and a little smelly. But their actual apartment was nice. Akira worked hard and did the best she could with their space. When they moved in, she and Marnyke scrubbed the whole thing, top to bottom. It was clean and all theirs. It was the first place they had ever had, just the two of them.

Marnyke took the rickety elevator to their apartment on the twenty-first floor. She hoped Akira would be home, but didn't expect her to be. Akira worked at two restaurants downtown. She worked every night at one joint or the other. "The best money is at dinner," Akira would say. "Dinner is more expensive, so the tips are better."

Marnyke unlocked the door and turned on the lights. Of course, Akira was not there. Marnyke dropped her bag and jacket on the couch and glanced at the coffee table. A letter from the school was there, propped up against a candle.

Marnyke knew her sister had put it there. The letter was unopened, and it was from the guidance office. "That can't be anything good," she thought. She grabbed the letter, walked into her bedroom, and tossed it on her bed. Then she took off her dress and tossed it on the bed too. She walked to the bathroom and started the bathtub.

Don't cost a thing to take a bath. That's what her mom used to always say anyway. Her mom always took a bath before a big date. She had a lot of big dates, Marnyke supposed. To the best of her memory, it seemed like Marnyke's mom lived in the damn bathtub.

Marnyke sat on the edge of the tub with her hand under the running water. It took a while to get hot water on this floor. As she waited, her mind went back to the letter. It was probably about her grades. Or maybe her absences. It was nothing good, she knew that.

When the water was finally warm, Marnyke put the plug in and walked back to her bedroom. She looked at the letter on the bed. If other kids her age got a letter like that, their parents would open it right away and flip out.

But Marnyke didn't have parents. She had her sister Akira. And Akira had simply set the letter on the coffee table for Marnyke to open herself. Marnyke walked back to the living room and got the magazine out of her bag. She brought it into the bathroom and set it by the tub.

She stepped into the water. The back of her right heel burned a little. But Marnyke knew the hot water would be good for it. She slowly bent her long legs and sat down in the tub. Marnyke didn't let her hair get wet though. She was going to meet up with Darnell, and her hair was looking good today. She wanted to keep it that way. She needed all the help she could get these days.

Lately Darnell just didn't seem as interested in her as he used to be. More and more, Marnyke felt that he was slipping away. But Marnyke wasn't going to let that happen. Not without a fight anyway. Darnell was a catch, and Marnyke intended to do everything she could to keep him.

Marnyke sat up in the water and reached for the fashion magazine. She carefully scrutinized the bodies of every female on each page, comparing herself to the models. She thought, "This one has a better chest. My legs are way better than hers. Her skin is better than mine." By the time she was finished going through the thick magazine, the water was almost cold.

After pulling the plug out, Marnyke stood up. She dried herself off, wrapped the towel around her skinny frame, and walked into her bedroom. She threw the wet towel on the letter and turned to her closet.

What she really needed was a cute outfit. Her right heel was destroyed, so her shoe options were limited. Marnyke looked for a bandage, but all she found was an empty Band-Aid box in the medicine cabinet. Frustrated, she tossed the box in the trash.

Black dress, black boots, she decided. Her old standby. The boots would be easy on her heel. Plus, the tight, slinky black dress hugged all the right parts of her in all the right ways. She'd always had good luck with that dress. It had worked magic before. Hopefully it would tonight too.

Marnyke got dressed and looked in the mirror. She liked the way she looked. She felt better already. She added some big hoop earrings and lipstick. Then she grabbed a pack of cigarettes from her dresser and headed for the door.

On the way, she picked up her jacket off the couch and put it on. She put the cigarettes in a pocket. Marnyke never took cigarettes to school. It was too risky. But she always carried them at night when she went out. They were a lot easier to get now that Darnell was eighteen. He could buy them for Marnyke whenever she had the money, even though he didn't like doing it. She figured she better hang onto that man, if for no other reason than smokes.

Marnyke walked out of her apartment and locked the door. "I'll be home when I feel like it," she said sarcastically to no one. Then she went down twenty-one floors to the street. It felt good to be outside. She pulled out a cigarette and searched for a lighter. Oh, crap. She forgot to grab one! That's when she heard a familiar, annoying voice.

"Haven't seen that dress in a while. You got business tonight or what?"

"Shut your face, Jackson," Marnyke said. "You got a light? Or you just gonna stand there and stare?"

Jackson said, "Sorry, I ain't got a light." He looked her up and down. "Always liked that dress," he said.

"I know," Marnyke smiled. She put the cigarette back in the pack.

"You meetin' Darnell?" Jackson asked.

"Who else?" Marnyke answered. "I gotta run. Peace." She could see Jackson on his phone instantly, texting everyone. "What a jerk," she thought.

Marnyke walked away, hips swinging in her signature way, heading back to the subway.

[chapter]

2

Marnyke got off the train at the Northeast stop. Darnell lived in Northeast Towers, a few blocks away. He lived in one of the towers. Kiki lived in the other, with her parents and twin sister, Sherise.

Marnyke climbed the stairs up to the street and headed toward Darnell's place. Suddenly, she stopped and looked back toward the subway entrance. She had this funny feeling that Jackson may have followed her. You never knew when that fool might decide to do something like that. But she didn't see Jackson. Instead, she saw some other fool, a young punk she had never seen before in her life.

"You lookin' hot, girl. You lookin' for me, I hope?" the young man said.

"Do I know you? I don't think so. Get up out of my face," Marnyke snapped.

The man scowled at her and held up both his hands. "So fine, but so foul," he said. "Damn, girl. Take it easy." Then he shook his head and continued walking down the street.

Marnyke took a few more seconds to scan the mess of people near the stop. But she didn't see Jackson. So much for her funny feeling. She rolled her eyes and turned back toward Darnell's.

But the closer she got to Darnell's building, the more nervous she became. She wanted a smoke, but then her breath would be all nasty when she saw Darnell. She'd just have to wait until she left his place.

At least her boots were easy to walk in, and they didn't hurt her sore heel. They looked good with her dress too.

But wait. Would she take her boots off when she got to Darnell's? No. She should leave 'em on. She didn't want her heel to bleed all over the place, since she didn't have a damn bandage on it. Plus, the boots were hot. And it wasn't like Darnell's place was all that clean anyhow.

Would Darnell even notice how good she looked? Marnyke hoped so. Not that long ago he would have for sure. These days, however, Marnyke couldn't be sure. Had he gone too soft now? Had things changed that much?

Darnell practically grew up on the street. He was deeper into the gang scene than any of the other guys at school Marnyke knew. But about two years ago, Darnell left all that behind and cleaned up his act.

———

He made basketball his life. He lived for South Central basketball season. In fact, he was the best player on the team. True, the season was over now. And the team hadn't done so great. But Darnell did get a scholarship. It wasn't to the school he wanted, and it wasn't a full ride either. But still, it was a good opportunity for a guy who used to be nothing but a thug.

Point is, Darnell had his life together now, and Marnyke was gonna hang onto him for dear life. If only she could get him back where she wanted him.

To hell with her breath. Marnyke reached into her jacket for a cigarette. She put one up to her lips and then remembered that she didn't have a lighter.

Marnyke looked around for someone with a light. She walked by an alley and saw some lit cigarettes in the dark. But those guys were speaking Spanish.

Marnyke didn't want to ask them. So she kept walking. Soon she was a block from Darnell's. She tried to put the cigarette back in her pack, but it broke. She threw the pieces onto the sidewalk.

Marnyke stopped a moment in front of Darnell's building. She tried to pump herself up. "You can do this. He wants you. You know he does. Keep it together," she told herself. She pressed the buzzer. She waited for what seemed like forever.

"What up," Darnell's voice finally came through the crackling intercom.

"Hey," Marnyke said. "You gonna let me in or what?"

The door buzzed loudly. Marnyke opened it and went inside. Darnell's building didn't smell any better than hers did. From the entryway, Marnyke could smell a variety of foods cooking. All together, it didn't smell very good. But it did make Marnyke hungry. She hadn't eaten anything since lunch, and she highly doubted she'd get anything to eat at Darnell's.

She made her way up to Darnell's floor and down the hall. She noticed that the door was open. Darnell must have opened it after he buzzed her in. Marnyke felt shaky, but she tried to stay focused. She was here on business, you could say. The business of keeping her man.

Marnyke opened the door slowly and heard familiar noises. Darnell was playing last year's Madden, his favorite PlayStation game.

Marnyke realized that's why he left the door open. He didn't want to have to pause his game again to let her in. Darnell got so into those damn games, especially since basketball season ended. "So much for me gettin' any attention," Marnyke thought.

Darnell didn't get up when she entered. He was sitting in an old recliner. It was right in front of the television. "What up, Marnyke," he said. "Girl, I'm about to kill this guy. Check it out." Marnyke looked around the apartment. It didn't seem like Darnell's mom was home.

"Your mom at work?" Marnyke asked.

"Huh? Ah, yeah. I think so."

Marnyke took a deep breath, though she tried not to make it too loud. Then she walked across the kitchen floor. Her heels clicked rhythmically on the dirty linoleum. The sound disappeared when she hit the living room carpet. She stopped right behind Darnell's chair.

"I hope you remember where the pause button is," she whispered into Darnell's ear.

"Oh, yeah?"

"Yeah," Marnyke replied. Darnell paused the game.

Marnyke walked around his chair and stood in front of him. "Well?" she said, putting her hands on her hips. "Do I look like more fun than Madden or what?"

Darnell smiled. "You sure do," he said, leaned toward her until he was at the front edge of the recliner's seat. Then he reached out to touch her hips. "What you dressed so fine for anyhow?"

"For playing video games with you. What else?" Marnyke said. She was glad he had put his hands on her. It's what she wanted him to do. Still, she felt nervous. But she pushed on, smiling and reaching out to touch his face.

"You happy to see me tonight, Darnell?" she asked.

Darnell smiled. He pulled her closer to him. "For real," he said.

Marnyke raised her eyebrows. Darnell tried to pull her in even closer to him, but she resisted. "You sure you're happy to see me?" she asked again. "No one else you'd rather have with you right now?"

For a split second, a second so short Marnyke couldn't tell if it was real, she thought he hesitated.

"You're straight up crazy," Darnell said. "Come here." Then he pulled her in toward him again. This time, Marnyke did not resist. He kissed her hard, and she kissed him hard right back. She let herself go. It felt so good to have his affection. It made everything better. When Darnell picked her up, she didn't know where they were going, and she didn't care.

Darnell carried Marnyke to the couch and set her down. He was on top of her now, and everything was happening quickly. Marnyke was so in the moment that she didn't stop kissing him, not even when she heard the sound of keys jingling near the door.

She really hoped it wasn't his mom. Not now. It couldn't be. Darnell said she was at work.

For his part, Darnell ignored the sound too, as long as he could. But when he heard the key in the lock, he sprang up off of her. Usually, Darnell's movements were fluid and smooth. The man was an athlete. But as went back to the recliner, he looked uncoordinated and awkward. When he picked up the controller, it looked like his hands were shaking.

Marnyke didn't do much better. She sat up on the couch in a clumsy rush. She then tried to adjust her dress down into a somewhat normal place. She knew that her hair was a disaster. No doubt she looked a fool when Darnell's mom walked through the door. "Hey, Ms. Watson," Marnyke said.

"Hello," Darnell's mom replied. She looked very tired. She was holding a bag of groceries. "Hi, baby," she said to Darnell.

"Hi, Mom," Darnell said.

"I was just on my way out," Marnyke said. "Good to see you, though."

"You too, young lady." Darnell's mom said.

Then Darnell's mom headed slowly to the kitchen. Marnyke stood up quickly. She didn't want to waste any time. She headed for the door, stopping just behind Darnell's recliner. She put her hand on his shoulder. "See ya tomorrow," she said softly.

"Later, Marnyke," Darnell replied.

When Marnyke opened her eyes the next morning, she felt tired. She wanted to stay in bed. She sure as hell did not want to go to school. But she had to. The school was sending letters, after all. She had to show. Besides, it was Friday. Just one more day.

Marnyke rode the train to South City and then walked to South Central High. She was running a little late, so she picked up the pace. She wanted to talk to Kiki before first period.

Darnell was waiting at her locker. When she saw him, her heart began to race. There was one good reason to come to school. To see a man as fine as Darnell waiting for you at your locker. What was on his mind? Marnyke had no idea. But Darnell knew what he wanted to say. And he didn't waste any time getting to the point.

"Girl, were you trippin' last night? Or were you for real? You came on like you wanted somethin'. Somethin' you've never seemed to want so bad before," Darnell said.

Marnyke looked around to see if anyone could hear this all go down. But there was hardly anyone in the hall because class was about to start any minute.

"What you playin' at, Marnyke?" I gotta know what's up with you," Darnell continued.

Marnyke was surprised by how clearly he said what was on his mind. Darnell was a hell of a ball player. But the man wasn't much with words. He usually had a hard time speaking. Sometimes he even stuttered. But not this morning. This morning he was speaking his mind just fine.

"Darnell, I'm ready to—" The bell rang, interrupting her.

Darnell didn't budge. He stared hard at Marnyke. "You sure?"

Before Marnyke could answer, Mr. Crandall saw them. "Move it, you two," he said. Mr. Crandall was the world's worst guidance counselor. Marnyke never liked running into him. And she certainly didn't like seeing him right then.

Marnyke touched Darnell's arm. "I'm sure," she replied quietly.

"I said move it," Mr. Crandall repeated.

Darnell glared at Mr. Crandall. Then his eyes came back to Marnyke's. "We'll finish this at lunch," he said. Marnyke nodded. Then they parted ways.

Marnyke didn't listen to a word of anything all morning. All she could think about was Darnell. She had his attention now, all right. And it felt great.

Marnyke had science fourth period. She didn't really like science, but at least she had that class with Kiki. She couldn't wait to tell her all about last night. She was anxious for Kiki's take on it.

Mr. Colbe, the science teacher, said that they would be doing a lab today with partners. What luck! Naturally, Marnyke and Kiki teamed up together. Mr. Colbe explained the project. It was something about weight and mass. Marnyke didn't really get it. But she rarely understood what Mr. Colbe was saying.

She and Kiki went to a lab table. "Kiki, get this," Marnyke started. "It almost happened. Last night! Me and Darnell."

"For real?" Kiki replied.

"For real. Problem is, his mom came home! Right in the middle."

Kiki's jaw dropped. "No way. How embarrassing!"

"I know, right?" Marnyke replied.

"So you still feel good about this? Still feel like he's the right guy and all?" Kiki asked.

"Damn straight," Marnyke replied. "I totally trust him."

Kiki nodded. It looked like she had something more to say but stopped herself. Then she turned her attention to the lab sheet.

"So what you doin' this weekend?" Marnyke asked. Kiki finished weighing a liquid. As she recorded the weight, she let out a big sigh.

"Well, big family dinner on Sunday. And there's a Northeast Meet-Up on Saturday," she explained.

"Oh, damn! I forgot about that. Your stepdad is all up in that stuff, isn't he?"

"Oh yeah," Kiki replied. "Way into it. He thinks he's, you know, saving the hood and everything."

Kiki's stepdad was in charge of Northeast Meet-Up, a project to raise money for improving the community. They had Meet-Ups about once a month. There was always food and music. Usually dancing too. Kiki's stepdad was really active in the community. He loved the northeast part of the city, even though most of it was pretty run-down these days.

"You don't sound too excited about the Meet-Up," Marnyke said.

"Not as much as Sherise is," Kiki explained. "She lives for that crap. It's a chance for her to play dress-up and hold a microphone. You feel me?"

Kiki and Sherise were twins, but they were nothing alike. Kiki was good at sports and school. She was like a super-smart tomboy. Sherise, on the other hand, was, well, prissy. She was good at looking good.

Marnyke nodded. "I feel you. Sherise does like to dress up. But, a girl's gotta dress sometimes."

"I know," Kiki said. "But get this. I asked Sherise if I could borrow an outfit. You know, just for the Meet-Up. She was all, 'Well, I don't know. You can wear this but not that.' She's got more clothes than anyone I know! Girl can't even share with her own sister?"

"What you lookin' to wear, Kiki? You know I got tons," Marnyke said.

Kiki blushed. "I don't know. I just wanna look good, you feel me?"

Marnyke smiled. "Girl, you come over to my place before the Meet-Up. You can wear anything of mine you want. I'll help you put the perfect outfit together."

Kiki was thrilled! "For real, Marnyke? That would be so cool. I love your clothes!"

"We'll have you lookin' so fine every man at South Central will want you. That's probably why your sister don't want you in her stuff. She knows you'll look better than she does in 'em!"

Kiki smiled and looked down. "Yeah, right," she said.

"So who's your sister chasing these days anyway? She got her sights on anyone?" Marnyke asked.

"She hasn't mentioned anyone," Kiki said. "All she cares about these days is the Meet-Up. She's so hyped. She says the music is going to blow everyone away."

"Well, Kiki, we'll have you in some threads that will blow everyone away too!" Marnyke said with a smile.

She meant it too. She liked Kiki. Kiki was so sweet and straightforward. They had become good friends through year-book club. Marnyke was happy to lend her some clothes.

Kiki took another measurement and filled in another answer. She set her pen down and looked at Marnyke. "Hey, do you have plans Sunday? Wanna come over for dinner?"

Marnyke hesitated. She went there a while ago and felt pretty awkward. After all, family get-togethers are for families. And she wasn't family. Plus, the twins' stepdad was so damn straight. It made Marnyke uncomfortable. "We'll see, okay, Kiki? I gotta talk to my sister first," Marnyke finally said.

Kiki nodded and smiled. Then she continued with the worksheet. Marnyke announced that while Kiki did the work-sheet, she'd think about outfits for her for the Meet-Up. Moments later, they were rudely interrupted.

"Hi, Kiki!" squealed a voice that Marnyke had come to dislike a great deal. It was Tia, yearbook club manager. Tia was so annoying! She was always trying to use people to get an edge. If you couldn't help her get ahead, she wanted nothing to do with you. Marnyke didn't trust her.

Tia walked right up to their lab table. "Guess what I'm holding!" Tia squealed again.

Kiki smiled. "Is that the yearbook? Are they in already?"

"Well, yes, they are. They're not handing them out until after lunch though. I got the first copy because, well, I'm the manager. You were a big part, *chica*. You did such a great job laying out the pages. We couldn't have done it without you! You worked hard on the yearbook, so I wanted to give you an advance copy too."

"Got one for me?" Marnyke joked.

Tia rolled her eyes. "I'm only giving advance copies to important members of the yearbook club. Not slackers who are only a part of YC because they got too many absences and don't want to be kicked out of school."

"*Muchas gracias*, Tia," Kiki said. Tia glared at Marnyke and walked away. Marnyke scowled after her.

"How come you don't like Tia?" Kiki asked. "You should be nicer to her. That girl is gonna take over the world some day. You'll want to be on her good side when she does."

Marnyke just rolled her eyes, as Kiki examined the hot-off-the-press yearbook.

"The cover looks pretty sweet," Kiki said, holding the yearbook in her hands. She opened it up and reviewed the inside cover. "Nice color too."

Kiki then turned to the first page of the yearbook. Marnyke heard her gasp. "What's the matter?" Marnyke teased as she doodled on their worksheet. "They put a picture of Mr. Crandall's bare white butt in there or somethin'?"

Kiki looked nervous. "No, nothing like that," she said timidly.

"Well, what? A mistake?" Marnyke asked, sliding over to Kiki's side of the lab table. That's when she saw the photo. It really was a hell of a photo. It was in color and almost a whole page. It showed Darnell in a sweet embrace. He was all smiles, squeezing someone with both arms. The only problem was, he wasn't squeezing Marnyke. He was squeezing Sherise. Prissy, perfect little Sherise.

"Nice photo," Marnyke said. "You choose that one, Kiki? Thanks tons."

Kiki shook her head. "No way, Marnyke. That wasn't there in the last layout I saw.

For real. I can't remember exactly what was there. But it wasn't this. I'm sure of it."

Marnyke believed her. But that didn't take away the burning in her stomach and chest. Marnyke imagined the whole school getting their yearbooks after lunch. By this afternoon, everyone in the whole school would see it and be talking about it.

She couldn't bear it. Marnyke knew she had to get out of there. She didn't want to stand Darnell up at lunch. But she just couldn't be there when everyone was opening up to that first page of the yearbook.

"I gotta dip," Marnyke said to Kiki. "If Mr. Colbe asks, tell him I got cramps super bad or somethin'. Just cover for me, okay?"

Kiki looked sad. "You sure, Marnyke?" she asked. "We can go to lunch together and—"

"I'm okay, Kiki. Really," Marnyke interrupted. "It's just a stupid photo. Come on girl, you know me. I can't ever stand a full day in this school. I'll hit you up later."

Marnyke grabbed her things and slipped out of the science room without a sound. She'd never wanted to get out of school so bad in her life. A rage so deep ran through her that she didn't know what else to do but run.

Darnell waited impatiently in the cafeteria. He was anxious to talk to Marnyke. He wanted to know what was going on with her. He needed to know now, before he graduated, if they had something or not. The truth was that he just wasn't sure. When they first started dating, Darnell was so happy. He couldn't believe Marnyke wanted to date him! He'd waited his whole life to get a girl like Marnyke. And out of the blue, she liked him. She wanted to be his girl.

But sometimes Darnell felt like she didn't really care about him. She just cared about his scholarship. He knew Marnyke had a rough life. He knew she wanted to be taken care of. But he just wasn't ready for that kind of responsibility. Maybe someday, but not now.

Darnell watched Sherise, Nishell, and Kiki come in and sit down together. Sherise made eye contact with him and smiled. Darnell smiled back. Sherise was a good girl. Too good for him by far. She came from a good family and stayed out of trouble. Still, Darnell liked how she didn't seem to care about him because of basketball. She seemed to care more that they liked the same kind of music.

They both liked the same kind of music. Mostly blues and hip-hop. Music that really had something to say. You could say that Sherise liked good music like Marnyke liked vintage clothes.

Where was Marnyke anyway? Darnell looked at his watch. The lunch hour was half over. He couldn't believe it. She was standing him up. Couldn't that girl stay a whole day in school for once? Just once? Especially since they had business? Darnell grabbed his tray and went to sit with Jackson.

Jackson looked surprised to see him. "I thought you and Mar had to talk?" Jackson asked. "What happened?"

"Girl can't even give me her time," Darnell said, shaking his head.

"I don't know what to tell you, man," Jackson replied. "Girl makes up her own rules."

"What's that supposed to mean?" Darnell asked.

"I'm just sayin'," Jackson replied, "that I know Marnyke. I know how she operates."

"Yeah? And how's that?"

"Look, she's just a hard one to figure. She's fickle. That's all I'm sayin'. She probably saw that photo of you and Sherise in the yearbook and decided she didn't want to see you no more."

Darnell was confused. "What photo?"

"You'll see it," Jackson said. "It's on, like, the first page, dawg. It's of you and Sherise. And you're holdin' on to her like you don't ever want to let her go."

Darnell couldn't remember taking any photo with Sherise. "For real?" he asked.

"For real," Jackson replied. "Marnyke ain't gonna take that lyin' down, man."

Darnell looked down at his plate. "Me and Sherise," he said, "we're friends. That's it. Marnyke should know that."

"If she knows that, then why ain't she here?" Jackson asked. "She's probably burning down your house or somethin' right now."

It's true that Jackson knew Marnyke pretty well. But he was wrong about where she was at that moment. She wasn't burning anything down. Quite the opposite actually. She was crying her eyes out.

Marnyke felt terrible. Absolutely awful. She didn't cry on the subway ride home. And she didn't cry all the way up to the twenty-first floor of her building. But when she opened the door and saw that she was alone, she let it all out. She flopped down on her bed and the tears burst out of her.

She knew that by the end of the day, the whole school would see the picture and be talking. Everyone would know that Darnell didn't really care about her. Marnyke had known that for some time. But now the whole school would know, and Marnyke couldn't take it any longer.

Everything was bad. Why was this happening? Who put that damn photo in the front of the yearbook? Probably

Sherise. That prissy little skank! She was YC president, after all.

Marnyke had never known her to have a nasty side, though. And putting that photo there at the last minute was certainly wicked. Marnyke's tears drenched the sheets on her bed. But she didn't move her head. Not even when the phone rang. Marnyke let it go to the old-school answering machine.

"Hi, this is Mr. Crandall from South Central High. I'm calling about Marnyke. It seems she has left school for the day without permission. Also, this is her eighteenth unexcused absence this semester. I'm going to need to meet with Marnyke and one of her parents first thing Monday morning to discuss our next steps."

Marnyke lifted her head from the wet sheets. She walked to the answering machine and deleted the message. Then she went back to her bed and fell fast asleep. Maybe everything was just a bad dream. Maybe it would be better after she slept on it for a while.

Marnyke woke up to her sister's hand on her back. "Girl, what you doing home already?" Akira said, sitting down on Marnyke's bed. "You cut class? It's only 2:00! You gotta stop skipping! Is that what that letter from the school is about?" Slowly, Marnyke turned over onto her back. Akira saw her sad, red eyes. She instantly felt for her sister.

"Marnyke! What is wrong? Are you okay? What happened?" Akira asked.

Marnyke put her head on Akira's leg. "Everything is wrong," Marnyke started. "I don't think Darnell likes me anymore."

"Hush now," Akira said. "What makes you think that?"

"Because he likes this perfect little ... slut instead," Marnyke cried.

Akira asked, "What perfect little slut? Who are we talking about?"

"That's the worst part," Marnyke cried. "It's Sherise. He likes Sherise. Prissy little perfect Sherise."

"Sherise? Come on, Marnyke. Sherise doesn't really seem like Darnell's type."

"You're wrong," Marnyke said. "The yearbook came out this afternoon. There's a picture of them hugging, right on the first page! Everyone at school is laughing behind my back by now for sure. They look so cute together. What am I going to do?"

Telling Akira about the yearbook made Marnyke lose it again. She was a girl on the edge of a big-time breakdown. Her whole body shook as she cried into her sister's lap.

Akira said, "I'll tell you what we're gonna do. We're gonna go to Seventh Street. That's what we're gonna do. Get up and get ready. I got about fifty extra bucks. You can get whatever you want."

"No way," Marnyke said. "I'm not buying clothes with your money. You buy everything else around here. You don't need to be doing that for me."

Akira opened her purse. "No, for real! Look. I had this table today. About eight guys. They knew the owner. Anyhow, they were big tippers. What, you think I'm gonna buy myself something hot? I'm about to be an old married lady soon. I don't need that stuff. Sounds like you do, though."

Marnyke rolled her eyes. "You're not gonna stay married long if you look like hell all the time," she said.

"I know that," Akira said. "But I want to buy you something. It's been forever. Come on. Let's see if they got anything good. But you better wear your sunglasses. Your eyes look like hell, girl."

Marnyke laughed. "Okay," she said, sitting up. "Let's go check it out. Whatever extra you got to spend, we'll split it. How about that?"

Akira shook her head. "Tell you what. You start buying the Band-Aids around here. I see you went through another box. You burn through those things like nobody's business. You gotta start taking better care of your feet, Mar! Really!"

This made Marnyke laugh. "Okay, I'll start buying the Band-Aids," she said.

Akira and Marnyke walked to the discount store on Seventh Street. Marnyke loved that store more than any other in the whole world. But she loved spending time with her sister even more. They used to spend every second together. But it wasn't that way anymore.

Marnyke sometimes blamed Akira's fiancé Ashon for that. He was a good-enough guy. The three of them all got along pretty well. Plus, Ashon helped Akira financially when he could. In fact, Ashon helped Akira with the security deposit on their apartment. It was the first time Marnyke could ever remember a man helping out.

But Ashon took up a lot of Akira's time. He had a big family, and ever since they got engaged, it seemed like Akira was going over there more and more. Akira always invited Marnyke to join them. But it never felt right to Marnyke. She wasn't the one marrying Ashon. Akira was.

There wasn't much Marnyke could do about that. Akira was twenty-two now. A grown woman. Of course she wanted to be with her man. A woman can't spend all her free time with her little sister, after all. It just wasn't the way of things. Still, Marnyke wondered where that left her.

"What's gonna happen, anyway? Once you two are married?" Marnyke asked.

"What, you think we're gonna kick you out?" Akira joked.

Marnyke looked down at the sidewalk. "You tell me," she replied.

Akira put her arm around Marnyke. "Nothing," Akira said. "Nothing is going to change. It's been me and you for a long time now. That's the way it's gonna stay. Until your skinny butt becomes a famous model and you buy me my first house."

Marnyke smiled and put her head on Akira's shoulder. "Sounds like a plan," she said.

At the discount store, Marnyke and Akira each grabbed a few things. Then they headed into one dressing room together.

"I'm trying this on first," Marnyke said, holding up a red, seventies-style jumpsuit. It was low-cut in the front with straps that tied behind the neck. She quickly put it on.

"Damn!" Akira said. "You look fly as hell in that, Mar! You got a strapless bra to wear with it?"

Marnyke shook her head no.

"It's cool. You can wear mine. Might be a little big for ya though!" Akira joked.

"Shut up!" Marnyke smiled. She liked the outfit too. But she wasn't sure about the back, where it tied at the neck. "Akira, what about back here. Can you see it? The scar?"

"It's fine, Mar," Akira said, gently placing her hand on the scar. "The straps cover it right up."

Akira and Marnyke stood in front of the mirror. "You have her figure. You know that?" Akira said. "Her style too." This made Marnyke smile. "Mom didn't have much going for her," Akira continued. "But she sure knew how to dress."

Marnyke turned away from the mirror and faced her sister. "Akira, can we spend this Sunday together? Just me and you? We haven't had dinner together, just us, in forever."

"Yes, that sounds great. We should make dinner. I've even got the day off!" Akira said.

"You promise we can hang out?" Marnyke asked.

"I promise, but only if you quit ditching school. What, you trying to drop out or something? Get your head on straight, girl. Have you even learned anything this year?"

Marnyke laughed. "I know all there is to know," she joked. "But still, I'll quit skipping class so much just for you since you're throwing down on this hot outfit."

Marnyke and Akira took their things to the counter. Akira paid for a purple hat for herself and the jumpsuit for Marnyke. Then they walked back to their apartment.

"We're doing all right, us two," Akira said as they took the old elevator up to their floor. "A lot of girls in our situation would have lifted this stuff. You feel me?"

Marnyke nodded. "Yeah, we're doing all right," she replied.

Once in their apartment, Akira walked to the answering machine. "One message," she said as she pressed the button. Marnyke worried that it would be another message from Mr. Crandall. But it wasn't. It was from Darnell, and he never left messages.

"What up, Marnyke," Darnell's voice said. "I wanted to holler at you 'bout tomorrow night. I'm going to the Meet-Up early to help set up. But I hope to see you there whenever you get there. Peace."

Akira looked at Marnyke. "Now you got a hot outfit and a hot man for tomorrow night," she said.

"But the Meet-Up is Sherise's turf," Marnyke said. "And he didn't even mention the photo."

"Exactly," Akira said. "He probably didn't mention it because it doesn't mean anything to him."

Marnyke smiled. She loved her sister very much. Maybe Akira was right. Maybe everything was going to work out.

Marnyke woke up around noon the next day. Even though she was still tired, her mind was too busy to let her sleep anymore. The photo of Darnell and Sherise was still burning in her head. Was there something going on between them? Who put that photo on the first page anyway? Should Marnyke just play it off? Act like nothing? Or should she rip Sherise's perfect little eyeballs out?

Maybe she was overreacting. Maybe there was nothing going on with Sherise and Darnell. Why would Darnell be interested in Sherise anyway? She was too soft, too prissy. The girl relaxed her hair, for crying out loud.

Some guys must be into that kind of thing, Marnyke supposed. So many girls had that prissy style. It must work for some of them, right? But would that crap do it for Darnell? Marnyke shook her head. No way. He was more into girls with attitude, girls more like her.

Maybe it was all Sherise. Maybe she was interested in Darnell, but Darnell wasn't interested in her? Marnyke just couldn't be sure. The phone rang and broke into her crazy thoughts. It was Kiki.

"How you doin', girl?" Kiki asked.

"I'm cool," Marnyke replied. "What time you coming over?"

"How about now?" Kiki replied. "I figure you could use a friend. Besides, Sherise is driving me nuts. She's losing her mind over here. Meet-Up this, Meet-Up that."

"Sure, see ya soon." Marnyke agreed. Marnyke was glad that Kiki was coming over. She'd have someone to go to the Meet-Up with. Plus, maybe Kiki would have some answers. Kiki was Sherise's sister. Surely she knew something.

When Marnyke heard the old elevator stop on her floor, she ran to the door. "Hey, Kiki," she said.

"Hey, girl," Kiki replied. She held her arms out and walked toward Marnyke. "You doin' okay?"

"Yeah," Marnyke said. "Akira took me to that discount store on Seventh Street. I got a hot new outfit for tonight."

"Let's see it," Kiki said.

Marnyke held up the jumpsuit. "Hot damn," Kiki said. "That is dope. You're settin' the bar pretty high for the rest of us."

Marnyke smiled. "No worries. There's plenty more where this came from.

And it's all free and in my closet, girl!" The girls went through every stitch of clothing in Marnyke's closet. It was so much fun! Marnyke even forgot about Darnell for a while.

"I love this skirt, Mar. What do you usually wear with it?" Kiki asked. Marnyke dug through all her tops, looking for the right one. She handed one to Kiki. Kiki slipped it on with the skirt.

"Damn, Kiki!" Marnyke exclaimed. "That outfit is hot as hell on you! It's definitely a winner. Do you like it? You have to wear it!"

Kiki was all smiles. "Yeah, thank you, Marnyke. It's perfect. I can't wait to roll into the Meet-Up!"

"Who you dressin' up for anyhow?" Marnyke asked.

Kiki looked down and smiled. "You know that guy Sean? He's Jackson's cousin. He's a great basketball player. He's really shy, but I thought ..."

"He's cute, Kiki! Hell, yes I know who Sean is. He's gonna be all over you tonight!"

Kiki looked at herself carefully from all angles in the mirror. "Is it all about outfits, Marnyke? Is that why guys fall over my sister and not me?" Kiki asked.

Marnyke smiled. "Don't you change a thing, Kiki. You got your own style. Once you start trying too hard, then you gotta try hard every day. For real. Come on now. How much time does Sherise spend in the mornings? You really want to start relaxin' your hair? Puttin' on all that makeup?"

Kiki laughed. "No way. I'll stick with my braids, thank you very much! Sherise has straightened her hair since seventh grade! It's gonna start breakin' off, I swear."

Marnyke laughed too. But then she got quiet. "Kiki, I have to ask. Do you think there's somethin' going on with Darnell and your sister?"

Kiki looked Marnyke in the eye. "I asked her about it last night. She said there was nothin' going on with her and Darnell. I just don't know, Mar. But I do know this. Our stepdad would never let Sherise date Darnell. Never. He thinks Darnell is a gangbanger loser. And in his mind, once a thug always a thug."

Marnyke was intrigued. "That just ain't fair," she said. "Darnell's no thug. Not anymore he's not. Sure, he used to be pretty rough. But not no more. Don't get me wrong. He's not on my good side right now. But he's no loser."

"I know," Kiki said. "I know he's no thug. My stepdad just gets like that sometimes. He's so afraid of a 'bad community' rap, you know? Just forget I even said it. Besides, we better hurry up. The Meet-Up starts in less than an hour!"

The girls finished getting ready and headed to the Meet-Up. Marnyke was nervous. A lot of kids from South Central High would be there. Were they all going to clown her about that photo? Marnyke expected the worst.

"I don't wanna go in there, Kiki," she said.

"You're going. You can't just hide," Kiki said. "You look fabulous. Darnell's gonna flip when he sees you! Are you kiddin' me? Come on. Let's do this."

The girls walked into the Northeast Community Center. The place looked great! It was packed with teens too. The girls could hear an unbelievable MC rapping over a hot track. "Who is this?" Kiki yelled to Marnyke.

"I don't know, but I'm into it," Marnyke yelled back. The girls held hands and moved through the crowd. Marnyke had a few inches of height on Kiki. She saw the MC first. "Kiki," she said, squeezing her hand. "It's ... Darnell!"

Kiki stood on her toes and looked. "No way," she said. But sure enough, it was Darnell all right. Rapping his damn heart out on stage in front of more than one hundred people. Both girls were stunned.

"Damn," Kiki said. "He's good. You ever see him do this before?"

Marnyke was so shocked she could barely speak. "Never," she said. "He's usually, well, he gets hung up on his words sometimes." The whole crowd seemed mesmerized by Darnell's rhymes. He was really holding everyone's attention. Marnyke couldn't believe it.

Finally, Darnell dropped the microphone away from his lips. He turned his back toward the crowd and walked toward the turntables. The crowd went wild! The DJ smiled at Darnell and kept spinning. Then Darnell handed the mic to Sherise.

"Let's hear it for Darnell!" Sherise yelled into the microphone. The whole crowd cheered. Darnell was all smiles.

Sherise continued, "The first time I heard this man rap, I couldn't believe my ears. That was months ago! Darnell told me then that he could never get up here in front of y'all. But I guess he's not so shy after all! Let's give it up for Darnell!"

The crowd erupted again. Darnell looked at Sherise, and Sherise looked at him. Then they threw their arms around each other. This looked just like the photo in the yearbook. When they did, the crowd just cheered even louder. Marnyke felt dead inside. Marnyke squeezed Kiki's hand. "Well, I guess that settles that," she said.

"Marnyke, you don't know ..."

"Oh come on, Kiki, just look at those two," Marnyke said.

Kiki looked back toward the stage. Sherise and Darnell were still hugging. When they finally pulled away from each other, they stared lovingly into each other's eyes. She couldn't disagree with Marnyke. Not with the onstage lightning those two had shared.

"Looks like two people in love to me," Marnyke said. "I gotta get the hell out of here."

Kiki grabbed her arm. "Marnyke, wait. I'll go with you. I don't need to be here."

"No way, Kiki," Marnyke said. "Look who's headin' this way."

It was Sean, the hottie from the basketball courts. "Hey, Kiki," he said. "What up, Marnyke."

Both girls said hi. Kiki didn't know what to do. But Marnyke did. "Sean, you best ask Kiki to step out here before someone else grabs her," Marnyke said. "You feel me?"

Sean smiled. Kiki looked puzzled. "Text me later, Kiki." Marnyke winked. Then she made her way toward the door. Kiki wanted to follow Marnyke, but Sean grabbed her hand.

"You're looking fine tonight, Miss Nosy," Sean said. Kiki smiled, but felt sad as she watched Marnyke disappear into the crowd.

Marnyke was just about to the door when she ran into Mr. Nelson, the twins' stepdad. "Well, hello, Marnyke!" he said. "Haven't seen you for a while. Probably since dinner at our place a few months ago, huh?"

"Yeah, I suppose," Marnyke said.

"It's good to see you again. I'm glad you're here! Young people need this kind of thing. Keeps 'em off the streets and out of trouble. So tell me, you enjoying yourself here tonight? What did you think of that last act?"

Deep inside, Marnyke knew she shouldn't do what she was about to do. But she couldn't help it. It just came out. "What the hell do I think? Well, I think it was pretty damn good, Mr. Nelson. But I used to date Darnell. I had hoped he could turn his life around, but he's goin' back to his gangbangin' ways. Just thought I should warn ya, Mr. Nelson. I gotta run. See you 'round."

With that, Marnyke swung open the side door and bolted. A hallway led to the main exit. Marnyke heard her own running footsteps in the empty hallway. But wait. She never heard the door close behind her. She turned around to see Jackson, holding it open.

"Shut that door, Jackson," Marnyke spit.

"Only if you tell me where you're going lookin' so fine."

"I'm goin' home, Jackson," Marnyke replied.

"Me too," Jackson said. "This place is lame. I'll roll out with you."

—
[chapter]
6

Marnyke and Jackson walked away from the Northeast Meet-Up. Marnyke felt very sad, mad, and guilty all at the same time. She was happy to have some company, even if it was Jackson.

"So what shoes you wearin', Mar? Are we walkin' or takin' the train?" Jackson asked. "You tell me, girl. It's up to you."

"Let's walk," Marnyke replied quietly.

"You got it," Jackson said. Then the two of them walked several blocks without speaking. It had been a while since they had spent this much time together.

—

They used to hang out a lot. In fact, you could say they used to be together all the time. They both lived near Midtown. So it was always easy for them to get together. No doubt, they had drifted apart in the last few months.

That was mostly Marnyke's doing. In fact, it was all Marnyke's doing. She knew Jackson didn't want the distance between them. He didn't like it at all. If he had his way, they'd be together all the time. Marnyke was sure of it.

Jackson wasn't one to stay quiet for very long. He kept looking over at Marnyke, trying to get a read on her face. But as was often the case, he couldn't tell what she was thinking. "You look smokin' tonight," he said finally. "Get it at that place on Seventh Street?" Marnyke nodded. "It's a good one, Mar," he said, reviewing her body further. "A damn fine color too."

"You always had taste," Marnyke replied. "I gotta give you that at least. You always had a good eye when it came to clothes."

Jackson smiled. "It's always easy lookin' at clothes when they're on you, Marnyke," he said. Marnyke nodded in thanks. She even smiled.

Jackson looked closely at Marnyke's neck. "Covers up your scar too," he added. "Can't even see it."

"Yeah, Akira was with me when I tried it on. She said the same thing," Marnyke replied.

If any other man in the whole world had even mentioned her scar, Marnyke would be a wreck. But Marnyke was comfortable around Jackson.

It was kind of odd, actually. Maybe it was because Marnyke knew he cared for her a lot. Maybe it was because she no longer really gave a rat's ass what he thought anyway. Whatever the reason, Jackson knew all about her life and her scar. He knew how she got it and why. Jackson was probably the only other person besides Akira that knew the whole story.

They kept walking. Suddenly, Jackson asked Marnyke if she'd heard from her mom lately. The question took Marnyke by surprise and changed Marnyke's pace to a crawl. She shook her head.

"No, not since, well, forever. Not since that first place we got in Midtown, I guess."

"I'm sorry, Mar. Sorry to hear that," Jackson replied. Then he passed her a small flask. Marnyke took a long pull then handed it back.

"It's okay. Thanks for asking," she said, gasping after drinking the straight whiskey. "You're not tryin' to get me all drunk, are you, Jackson?"

"No way," Jackson said. "Why you gotta go and say somethin' like that, Marnyke? I like you as you are right this damn second."

"I think you like me drunk just fine too." Marnyke said.

"Mar, you can't blame that night all on me. It takes two to ... you know," Jackson said.

"Yeah, or one person shoving alcohol down the other one's throat," Marnyke snapped back. "Come on, Jackson. Don't front like that. Let's be real."

"I'm sorry you feel that way 'bout it," Jackson said. "It wasn't like that for me. For me, that night was perfect. I didn't see anythin' wrong with it. I wish ... I wish you would trust me again, Mar. I don't think it's fair for you not to trust me no more."

Marnyke didn't say anything. Her pace quickened. She wanted to trust Jackson again. It would be nice to feel that for him again. But she just wasn't sure.

"What do I have to do, Marnyke? To make you trust me again?" Jackson asked.

"I don't know, Jackson. Okay? Can we just walk together?" The two walked the rest of the way in silence. At Marnyke's building, Jackson lightly reached out and took Marnyke's hand. "Give it to me straight, Mar. When you gonna end things with Darnell?" Marnyke looked down.

"Come on, Mar. I forgive you, okay? I know why you took your chance with him. I mean, I'm no basketball star. He is. I'm a little crazy. He's not. I get it. Come on, girl. I just wanna know when do I get another chance?"

Marnyke looked him in the eye. "I don't know, Jackson. Okay? I'm going to bed now. It's been a really long day.

I'll holler at ya later. Thanks for walking me home. I appreciate it. I really do. It was good talkin' to you."

As she turned to go, Jackson spoke up again. "Mar?"

"What?"

"Did you and Darnell ... you know. Sleep together?"

Marnyke shook her head. "No, we didn't. Okay? Now go home, Jackson. Damn, why you gotta ask me somethin' like that right now? You gonna go and tell everyone?"

Then Marnyke turned and headed into her building. She took the elevator up to the twenty-first floor. It was hard to know how to feel about Jackson. He was such a wild card, so hard to figure out. Marnyke knew that he was the kind of guy to say one thing and then do another.

Still, it felt kind of good to talk to him again. They used to talk so much. Maybe she could trust him again. She would like to anyway. But not just yet.

Meanwhile, down on the street, Jackson reached into his pocket. His phone had been blowing up the whole time he was walking with Marnyke. He was glad Marnyke didn't hear it vibrating. Good thing he turned it on silent back before he left the Meet-Up.

Jackson had three missed calls and two texts from Tia. He read the first text. "Where the hell are u?"

Then he read the second one. "Tell me you did not just leave with Marnyke."

Jackson didn't listen to the voice mails from Tia. He just straight up deleted them. Then he texted Tia, "Sorry Tia. I'm still into Mar. Me and u gotta end things. Peace out."

Jackson slipped his phone back in his pocket. He was happy that he finally got to talk to Marnyke. And hey, at least she hadn't slept with Darnell. That was definitely a plus.

Jackson took a long pull from his flask. Before he pulled it away from his lips, Tia texted back. **"U R sick. I can't believe I changed that photo in the yearbook 4 U. Go 2 hell."**

Smiling, Jackson headed home. He felt good about the evening overall. His plans were going as expected.

Marnyke, on the other hand, was crying her eyes out in her bedroom. She felt terrible for telling Mr. Nelson that Darnell was a gangbanger. Worse yet, she felt terrible because Darnell didn't want her anymore. He wanted perfect little Sherise. She wondered if they were hooking up right at that very moment.

However, back at the Meet-Up, things weren't looking good for Darnell and Sherise.

The party was ending. There were only about twenty teens left. It was mostly the people cleaning up, including Mr. Nelson, Kiki, Sherise, Sean, and Darnell.

"Sean, with those ripped muscles, how about carrying these amps to the van?" Mr. Nelson asked.

"I can grab one of them," Darnell offered.

But Mr. Nelson stared at him with disgust. "No thanks, Darnell. You can go now. We got this. Thanks for your help. And great job up on stage tonight. You really had the crowd jammin'." Darnell frowned and looked at Sherise. She looked like she was about to start crying.

"I see how it is, Mr. Nelson," Darnell said. "I see how you feel. I get it. You don't even want me 'round carryin' amps. 'Nough said. I don't need this."

Darnell looked back to Sherise. Her eyes were tearing up and she was shaking just a little. "I guess that's that," he said, walking backwards. "Thanks for everythin', Sherise. I appreciate everythin' you did for me tonight. It was real."

Marnyke woke up with puffy eyes the next morning. Was it even morning anymore? She had no idea what time it was. She just felt awful. That's all she knew. At least she was going to spend the day with Akira today. She didn't want to be around anyone else.

Curling her whole body around a pillow, Marnyke tried to remember a family dinner with her mom. She couldn't remember one. Not even for the holidays or anything like that. She did remember following her mom around in the mall one time. It must have been almost Easter. There was a guy dressed up in a huge bunny costume near the food court. He gave Akira and Marnyke some candy.

At the time, Marnyke thought it was a miracle. But thinking back, the guy was giving candy to every kid who passed by. Maybe they got a little more because their mom was such a flirt. She had probably just finished lifting some clothes too. That's what she always did when she brought Akira and Marnyke to the mall.

Akira. That was the real miracle. They were going to spend the whole day together. Marnyke rolled over. She could sleep a little longer. Akira would wake her up when she got home after her brunch shift.

Marnyke's phone rang. It was over on the dresser. Marnyke grumbled and got out of bed to answer it, just in case it was Akira. But it wasn't Akira. It was Kiki.

"Hey, Mar," Kiki said softly. "How are you?"

"I'm alive," Marnyke said. "How did your night end up? How did things go with Sean?"

"Oh, it was good. It was great, actually," Kiki said.

"Cool," Marnyke replied.

"So, I don't suppose you want to come over for family dinner, huh?"

Marnyke laughed. "No thanks, Kiki. I'm in no mood to see your sister. Plus, I'm hanging out with Akira today. I can't wait. It's been a while."

"That's awesome," Kiki said. "I'm glad."

"Yeah."

"Hey, I have to tell you somethin'," Kiki said quietly. "It's Sherise. She's real upset. Last night my dad told her to stay away from Darnell, and she's been bawling ever since. Basically, I think you're right. She's into him."

"Tell me somethin' I don't know," Marnyke scoffed.

"Hey, she's my sister and all," Kiki said, "so that's all I'm gonna say."

"I know," Marnyke replied. "I'm goin' back to bed, okay? I'll see you tomorrow after my meeting with Mr. Crandall."

"What you have to meet with him for?"

"Absences," Marnyke replied. "Probably my grades too."

"Oh, Mar. You gotta ..."

Marnyke cut her off. "I know, Kiki. I know. Just don't go there right now. Not today, okay? I know you're right. I just can't talk about it today."

"Okay," Kiki said. "I'll see you tomorrow though, right?"

"Right."

"Oh, Marnyke. One more thing," Kiki said.

"What?"

"Word is that Tia put the photo in at the last minute," Kiki said. "She told several people at the Meet-Up last night, apparently."

"What a shocker," Marnyke said sarcastically.

"I know, but get this!" Kiki said. "Tia said it was Jackson's idea. She said he acted all interested in her, and then gave her the idea to change the picture. She said he made her think they'd hook up after she did it. And of course, she doesn't really like you anyway, so she had no problem throwin' you under the bus. I told you to be nicer to that girl!"

"Jackson ... that bastard," Marnyke said.

"For real," Kiki responded. "I guess he ended it with her last night, one day after the damn yearbook came out. Can you believe that? Tia was all upset about it."

Marnyke let out a large sigh. "I don't

think I can take anymore chitchat, Kiki," she said. "Seriously."

"I know," Kiki said. "I'm so sorry about all of this, Mar."

"I'm sure you are, Kiki. I'll holler at you tomorrow," Marnyke replied.

"Okay. Bye, Mar." Kiki said.

"Later, Kiki." Marnyke hung up. What a nightmare her life was. It had all happened so fast. She didn't know what to do other than head back to bed and just wait for Akira.

In the living room, Marnyke noticed a note on the coffee table. It was from Akira, as usual. The note said, "Hey, Mar! Hope last night went well. I'll be home around 2:00. How about we head over to Ashon's family's place for dinner? There will be plenty of food! Sound good? Love you, Akira."

No. That did not sound good to Marnyke. Not one bit. She didn't want to spend the day with someone else's family. She wanted to spend it with *hers*.

But it seemed that Akira was pretty much a part of Ashon's family now. That meant that Marnyke didn't have a family anymore. Not even a sister. Marnyke crumpled the note in her hand and let it fall to the floor. She closed her eyes and reached back and felt her scar.

Marnyke had been only seven. In the middle of the night, she heard a ruckus in her mom's bedroom. She walked out into the hall and saw Akira by their mother's bedroom door. She was holding a knife.

Akira was only twelve. She told Marnyke to go back in her room. But then they heard their mother scream. Akira burst into the bedroom. Marnyke did too. Akira pushed Marnyke behind her. Then with a shaky arm, Akira held out the knife and faced the man choking their mother.

The rest was blurry. The man came at Akira, and the knife fell, cutting the back of Marnyke's neck. Seeing the blood, the man ran off. Their strung-out mother followed him. Akira held a towel to Marnyke's wound and got her onto the subway and to the emergency room.

After that, Akira and Marnyke didn't live with their mother anymore. Instead, they went to live with their mom's sister.

The phone rang and Marnyke jumped. She thought maybe it was Kiki with more bad news. But it wasn't Kiki. It was Darnell.

Marnyke snapped, "What do you want, Darnell?"

"Damn," Darnell said. "I just want to talk to you. That's all."

"Why don't you call your perfect little Sherise," Marnyke said. "I'm not in the mood right now, Darnell."

Darnell went silent. Marnyke could hear music in the background.

"I don't want to talk to her," Darnell said softly. "I want to talk to you."

"That certainly wasn't the case last night, Darnell. I think you wanted to talk to Sherise all last night."

Darnell exhaled loudly. He sounded pretty beat up. "Look, Marnyke," he said. "I know you don't believe me. But what you saw last night. That's all ... that was just ... I mean, it's just music. That's all."

Marnyke didn't respond.

"I don't want Sherise," Darnell continued. "Not in that way."

"I'm no fool, Darnell. I saw you two last night. You can't lie your way out of this. What kinda fool you take me for, anyway?" blasted Marnyke.

"Marnyke, I'm sor—" Darnell didn't finish. It sounded like he was crying. Marnyke was glad. She wanted him to cry. She wanted him to feel as low as she had these past few days. "Just come over, Marnyke. Will you? Please? I'm alone, and I just ... I just want you to come over. I feel like hell, Mar. Please?"

Again, Marnyke did not answer. That's because she knew why Darnell was sad.

He was sad because Mr. Nelson blew him off last night. He was sad because he knew he couldn't be with Sherise.

"What's the matter, Darnell? Mr. Nelson didn't invite you over for a big family dinner? Didn't welcome you right into his little Northeast family?"

Darnell didn't say anything.

Marnyke kept going. "You're sad 'cause Mr. Nelson won't let you date Sherise. Admit it, Darnell. You're talkin' to me right now 'cause I can date you. That's 'cause no one cares what I do. But Sherise can't date you. And you know that now."

"Sherise can try to date me all she wants. But that doesn't mean I want her. I want you." Darnell answered.

Now Marnyke went silent. Was it possible? Possible that Sherise wanted Darnell, but he didn't want her back? Could that be the explanation? Marnyke wanted to believe it. She wanted to believe it with her whole heart.

"Let's pick up where we left off, Marnyke," Darnell said. "Remember? When you came over? In that black dress? Just come over in that black dress again. No way is my mom comin' home tonight. I know that for a fact. Just come over. Please."

Marnyke had to admit she did want to go. She did want to pick up where they left off. She could almost taste it. Besides, Akira was spending the day with her man. Marnyke should do the same.

In a way, Marnyke felt like she had won, like Darnell wanting her was a win. She had done it. She had her man back. Right where she wanted him. That would show Tia and that prissy Sherise. Jackson and the whole school too, for that matter. At the same time, the attention from Darnell was bittersweet. It was bittersweet because Marnyke did not believe it was real. She couldn't trust him ever again.

"I just want to hold you, Marnyke. That's all. Please. Me and you. We gotta look out for each other, 'cause we're all each other's got. It's that simple, Marnyke. We should be together. Me and you. You know it."

In that moment, Marnyke decided she didn't care about real. She just wanted to feel loved.

"All right, Darnell," she said. "I'll come over."

Marnyke hung up the phone and walked into her bedroom. Moving through the clothes hanging in her closet, she found the black, slinky dress she had worn to Darnell's earlier that week. She held it up and looked at it. Her secret weapon.

She wished she could take a bath. A bath would calm her down. Her mind was a total mess. If Darnell really did love her and not Sherise, then why didn't he get hold of her last night? Why didn't he look for Marnyke at the Meet-Up? Why did it seem that Marnyke was the very last thing he cared about last night? Marnyke pushed those questions out of her mind. It didn't matter. To hell with the truth. She wanted to keep her man. That's what she set out to do. And now she had him.

She got dressed and looked in the mirror. She liked the way she looked. It made her feel a little better. She put on the big hoop earrings and applied some lipstick. Everything exactly as it was that night. Well everything except for her bloody right heel.

Marnyke grabbed her cigarettes from her drawer, and remembered a lighter this time. She picked her jacket up off of the couch. As she walked out of the apartment, she said, "See ya later" sarcastically to no one. Then she closed and locked the door.

She took the elevator down twenty-one floors. Once on the street, she lit a smoke and headed for the subway. As she walked, she tried not to think. She didn't want to think about anything. She just wanted things to be the way things were. She wanted Darnell.

With her hand on the railing, Marnyke made her way down the stairs to the train. It was then that she heard a familiar but annoying voice.

"Marnyke," Jackson said. "How many times you gonna wear that dress this week? It's not like you to wear somethin' more than once."

"Leave me the hell alone, Jackson," Marnyke said. "I mean it." Marnyke hurried down the stairs into the station. She wished a train would hurry up and arrive so she wouldn't have to talk to Jackson. She couldn't deal with him right now.

"What?" Jackson exclaimed, following her down the stairs and into the station.

"What's wrong? I thought we were cool? Where are you goin'?"

"Where do you think," Marnyke snapped.

"Mar, please. Can't you see he doesn't care about you?"

"Oh, and you do?"

"Of course I do. I always have."

"Really?" Marnyke yelled at him, her voice echoing in the underground station. "Is that so? Well, then, tell me why the hell you put Tia up to that crap with the picture in the yearbook, huh? Did you do that for me? Or was it for you? You're messed up, Jackson. Just stay the hell away from me."

Marnyke walked to the turnstiles and paid her fare. Jackson chased after her, jumping over the turnstiles so he didn't have to pay.

"Marnyke, please," Jackson said. "I could see what was going on with Darnell and Sherise. I knew you couldn't 'cause

... you just ... you wanted it to work with him so bad. I didn't want him to hurt you. That's all Mar. I did it for you."

"You didn't do it for me. You did it for yourself!" Marnyke shouted. "I'm done with you."

The subway was pretty empty since it was Sunday. But still, there were enough people around to notice Marnyke and Jackson fighting. They were causing quite a scene.

"Marnyke, please. I love you baby. I know you love me too. You just don't know it yet."

"I don't need someone I don't know I love right now. And I certainly don't need someone I can't trust. Now get out of my face, Jackson. Or I swear, I will scream."

Jackson looked around. A few people were coming toward them, trying to figure out what was going on. So Jackson started backing away. A train was pulling into the station. It was the one headed to South City. Marnyke headed toward it.

"He doesn't love you, Marnyke," Jackson called out. "You know he's just playin' you. I wish you weren't so blind."

Marnyke got on the train and sat down. Jackson stood on the platform and watched as her train left the station. Marnyke watched him too, until she couldn't see him anymore.

She looked down at her legs and the black boots. Then she began to sob. She was the only one in the train car, so she let it all out. She cried for her mother. She cried for her sister who was probably wondering where she was. She cried because she couldn't trust Jackson, the only person who really seemed to watch her back.

Marnyke imagined Darnell, in his apartment waiting for her. She imagined how good it would feel to collapse in his arms right now. Marnyke dried her tears and watched her reflection in the subway windows. When the train stopped at the Northeast station, she got off and ran up the stairs to the street.

When she got to Northeast Towers, she started down the sidewalk to Darnell's building. Suddenly, she stopped. No doubt, being with Darnell would feel good. But she knew in her heart that she needed to be anywhere else instead.

Marnyke turned around and took the other sidewalk. The one that led to Kiki and Sherise's building. Marnyke felt a strange sense of calm. It was a feeling she had not had for some time. True, she was scared as hell. But she knew, somehow, that she was doing the right thing.

Marnyke stood in the lobby of Kiki and Sherise's building for what seemed like forever. "Just do it," she told herself.

"Just push the frickin' buzzer. That's all you have to do."

Marnyke lifted her finger up to the buzzer. She hesitated for a moment. Then she quickly pressed it.

Luckily, Kiki answered. "Hello?" she said.

"Hey, Kiki, it's me," Marnyke replied.

"Marnyke! I'm glad you changed your mind. Thanks for coming," Kiki said. "I'll buzz you in."

"No, please don't. I'm actually not here for dinner, Kiki. I just stopped by to talk to your stepdad real quick. Could you go get him? Ask him if he'll come down to the lobby for a minute?"

"Everything okay, Mar?" Kiki asked.

"Yeah, for real. Everything's gonna be fine," Marnyke answered.

"Are you sure you don't want to eat? We have so much food."

"Yes, I mean no. I just need to talk to your stepdad real quick. That's all, Kiki. Will you go get him for me?"

"Okay," Kiki said. "I guess I'll see ya tomorrow." The intercom clicked off. A few minutes later, Mr. Nelson stepped out of the elevator. He was carrying a covered plate.

"Hello, Marnyke," he said. "What can I do for you?"

"Hi, Mr. Nelson. I'm sorry to bug you during your family dinner," Marnyke began, looking down at the floor. "I just had to come clean with you on somethin'. You know how I said that Darnell went back to gangbangin'? Well, I lied. He isn't a thug at all. He's really turned his life around. I swear it's true.

"Please don't take what I said last night to heart. I was, ah, just upset and jealous. Darnell is in love with Sherise. And I wanted him to be in love with me.

That's all. I'm gonna go now. I'll see you 'round."

Marnyke turned quickly and headed toward the door as fast as she could.

"Marnyke, wait," Mr. Nelson called out. Marnyke turned around. "You're very brave, Marnyke. I make my own decisions about people. But I appreciate you stopping by. Thank you. Here, if you won't stay and eat with us, please take some food home." He handed her the plate.

Marnyke smiled at Mr. Nelson. She accepted the plate of food, then turned and headed home.

Once on the train to Midtown, Marnyke felt like a cloud had lifted. As it often did, the steady sway of the subway relaxed her. It felt good to be moving. Marnyke spotted what she thought might be a fashion magazine a few seats down. But she didn't have the energy to get up and look.

When she got home, Marnyke noticed that there were three missed calls on the answering machine. True, one of them may have been from Darnell. Maybe they all were. One could be from her sister too, she supposed. But Marnyke chose to ignore all of them. Instead, she drew a bath.

She went all-out this time. Candles, bubbles, the works. Then she slowly bent her long legs and slid into the warm water. She went all the way into the water, not worrying one bit about letting her hair get wet.

The next morning, Marnyke did not want to go to school. But when did she ever? She rolled over and squeezed her pillow.

Then for some reason, she thought about Kiki. What would Kiki say if she were here right now? Kiki would probably tell her to get up and go to school, especially since she was supposed to meet with Mr. Crandall.

As usual, Mr. Crandall had scheduled their meeting for "first thing" Monday morning. Why did he always have to catch people at the worst time like that?

Why couldn't they meet "first thing on Friday" or even "last thing on Monday?" The man just liked to make things difficult. Marnyke was sure of it.

Still, Marnyke rolled out of bed and stood up. She was already going to have detention for skipping Friday. She didn't need to skip Monday too. She had to go. She got ready and headed out the door.

As she was leaving, she saw another note on the coffee table. It was from Akira, no doubt, but Marnyke just did not have it in her to read the damn thing and get bitched at for not going to dinner with Ashon's family.

At school, Marnyke headed for her locker. Someone was there waiting for her. It was Sherise this time. Marnyke noticed that Sherise didn't look so good.

"Hey, Marnyke," Sherise said.

Marnyke whipped off her jacket and tossed it into her locker. "Sherise,"

Marnyke began. "I gotta be real with you. You're the last damn person I want to talk to right now. You feel me? I suggest you step the hell away from me before I lose my cool."

Sherise looked down. "I know, Marnyke. I just wanted to tell you that I'm sorry. That's all." Sherise looked terrible. Her hair was a mess, and her eyes were puffy and dark. She didn't look so prissy and perfect. She actually looked like crap.

"I shouldn't have taken that picture with Darnell," Sherise said. "No way. I was asking for trouble. And I got it. So we're even. Okay?"

Marnyke shook her head. "Sure, Sherise. Whatever. I don't really see how me and you are even. But I really don't have time to discuss that with you right now. I gotta go meet with Crandall."

With that, Marnyke slammed her locker and walked to Mr. Crandall's office.

As she passed her classmates, Marnyke noticed that no one was looking at her funny. She had assumed that they would. She figured everyone would look at her and think, "There goes Marnyke, the girl who can't keep a man." But really, it seemed no one even remembered or cared what happened Saturday night.

Marnyke walked into Mr. Crandall's office and sat down. She looked around at all the framed images of birds on his walls. She put her head in her hands and rubbed her temples. The last few days had been such hell. She didn't know if she could handle Crandall right now. When he walked in the door, Marnyke braced for the worst.

"Marnyke, I'd hoped I wouldn't see you in here again," Mr. Crandall said. "I thought you understood the school's attendance rules. Why did you skip school Friday?"

"I was having personal problems," Marnyke said. "Girl stuff. You know?"

"Yes, I heard," Mr. Crandall said, walking over to open the blinds in his office. He heard? What the hell did that mean? What was Crandall talking about? Marnyke gripped the arms of her chair.

"That's why I was late, actually," Mr. Crandall said. "I just spoke with the superintendent. Apparently, he met with your legal guardian. We are to excuse your absence on Friday due to a 'family emergency' it seems." Marnyke smiled. She couldn't believe it. Akira came through for her. Just like in the old days.

"Yes, that's right," Marnyke said. "A family emergency. And everyone in my family is female, you know. So a family issue is like girl stuff, you feel me?"

Mr. Crandall forced a fake smile. "Yes, I guess I feel you, Marnyke. Thanks for explaining that. Listen, your absences are unacceptable. I need you to put forth a real effort to come to school, Marnyke. Even when you have these 'girl problems' you still need to come to class. Or at the very least you need to bring in an excuse signed by your legal guardian."

Marnyke nodded.

"I assume by your nod that you 'feel' what I'm saying. You're free to leave, Marnyke. Please try to avoid more unexcused absences."

Marnyke dashed out of Mr. Crandall's office. She couldn't believe it. It was the first time she had stepped out of the office without getting detention! Maybe things were turning around after all.

Or maybe they weren't. As Marnyke stepped into the hall, she nearly ran into Tia. Tia looked at Mr. Crandall's office and then back at Marnyke. "In a little trouble, Marnyke?" Tia asked in a mean tone.

"No, I'm actually not, Tia. Thanks for asking," Marnyke replied. "Any thing else you dyin' to know?"

Tia glared at Marnyke. "Well," she said, "I have been meaning to ask you what you think of the yearbook."

Marnyke smiled. Because Marnyke was all legs, she had about five inches on Tia. She walked right up to her until she could look down her nose at her. Tia looked a little nervous.

"Honestly, Tia, I loved it. You did a really nice job, with the exception of one little photo. But, hey. No one is perfect. Not even you, I guess!"

Tia was so surprised she nearly fainted. "Thanks, Marnyke," Tia replied. "I'm glad you liked it. So, are you going to be in yearbook club next year too, then?"

"Oh yeah," Marnyke replied quickly. "For real. And I'm gonna make sure I see the final layout too. Right before it goes to the printer. You feel me?"

Tia nodded. "Yeah, Marnyke. I feel you."

"Good. I'll see you later," Marnyke said. Then she walked away, hips swinging in her signature way.